LOOK AND FIND
STREET FIGHTER II™

Illustrator/Illustration Coordinator
Jeff Rebner

Colorists
Ray Fehrenbach, Marcus David, Wally Lowe

Cover Inker
Dan Burr

Letterer
Kelly Hume

Illustration Script Developer
Robert Mizaki

Published by Louis Weber, C.E.O.
Publications International, Ltd.
7373 North Cicero Avenue
Lincolnwood, Illinois 60646

© 1994 CAPCOM CO., LTD.

All rights reserved. This book may not be reproduced or quoted in whole or in part by mimeograph or any other printed or electronic means, or for presentation on radio, television, videotape, or film without written permission from the copyright owners.

Manufactured in the U.S.A.

8 7 6 5 4 3 2 1

ISBN: 0-7853-0699-4

STREET FIGHTER II is a trademark of Capcom Co., Ltd.

Look and Find is a registered trademark of Publications International, Ltd.

CAPCOM

PUBLICATIONS INTERNATIONAL, LTD.